D1116999

Originally published as *Eekhoorn wordt grote zus* in Belgium and the Netherlands
by Clavis Uitgeverij, 2020
English translation from the Dutch by Clavis Publishing Inc., New York

Visit us on the Web at www.clavis-publishing.com.

Squirrel Is Going to Be a Big Sister written and illustrated by Sam Loman

ISBN 978-1-60537-631-8

This book was printed in February 2021 at Nikara, M. R. Štefánika 858/25, 963 01 Krupina, Slovakia.

First Edition
10 9 8 7 6 5 4 3 2 1

Squirrel
Is Going to Be a
Big Sister

Clavis
NEW YORK

Sam Loman

Mommy Squirrel has a very big belly.
There's a baby squirrel inside.
Squirrel helps Mommy with preparing the crib
and the baby supplies.

"Mommy?" Squirrel asks. "Soon, when the baby comes,
will you still think that I'm sweet?"
"Of course," Mommy says. "You and the baby
are both **the sweetest.**"

The next morning, Daddy enters Squirrel's room.
"Congratulations, big sister!" he shouts happily. "You've got a little sister."
Squirrel jumps out of bed and runs to Mommy and the baby.
"She's so tiny," Squirrel says. "And pretty," Daddy beams.

"Do you think Baby Squirrel is prettier than me?" Squirrel asks.
"Of course not," Daddy says.
"You and the baby are both **the prettiest**."

Ding-dong! Grandma and Grandpa are here. "Hi Squirrel," Grandma smiles. "Where's that pretty, sweet little sister of yours?" Squirrel half-heartedly points at the crib. Grandma doesn't even say that Squirrel is pretty and sweet like she always does.

"Take a look," Grandpa says.
He's holding a big present.
"For me?" Squirrel asks.
Grandpa shakes his head. "No, this is for the baby."
"Oh," Squirrel says disappointedly.
But grandpa doesn't even hear her.

Quietly, Squirrel leaves the house.
She sits down on the big oak branch near the front door.

"Congratulations on your sister!" Bunny shouts.
"Thanks," Squirrel mumbles.
Bunny looks surprised. "Don't you like having
a sister? I've got seven! You'll get used to it.
Can I see the baby? I've got a present for her."
Squirrel points at the front door.
"Right this way," she sighs.

"Where's that pretty little sister of yours?" Badger asks.
Squirrel nods to the front door.
"Go take a look," she says. "Bunny is there too."
Badger smiles. "Aren't you coming?"
Squirrel shakes her head.
"No, I want to sit down for a moment."

A tear rolls down Squirrel's cheek.
She should be happy to have a new sister,
but she feels sad instead.
"Why are you crying?" Fox asks.
"I'm afraid that everyone forgets about me
now that I have a sister," Squirrel sobs.

"Of course not," Owl hushes. "You feel like that right now, but the baby is new and that's why everybody wants to see her. Soon, she'll just be Baby Squirrel and you'll be her big sister. **Both equally pretty and sweet**."

Fox wipes away Squirrel's tears.
"Do you mind if we go take a look?" Owl and Fox ask.
"Of course not," Squirrel says. "I'll be right there."

Just when Squirrel stands up to go inside, Bear arrives.
"Hi big sister!" Bear shouts.
"Hello Bear," Squirrel says.
"I'm here for Baby Squirrel. Can I see her?"

Squirrel opens the door.
"Go on in," she says. "I'll be right there."

Squirrel starts to sob again.
What if Squirrel's best friend Bear thinks
the baby is **prettier and sweeter** than her?

Then, Squirrel feels a tiny hand on her shoulder.
"You didn't think that I forgot about you, did you?"
Bear smiles. "Here, I have something for you too."
Bear gives Squirrel a present.

The prettiest and sweetest big sister

Curiously, Squirrel opens the present.
It's a painting of Squirrel.
*The **prettiest and sweetest** big sister,*
it says underneath.

"You'll always be my **prettiest and sweetest** friend," Bear says.
Squirrel starts to blush.
She does feel quite **proud** because she's a big sister now.
"Come on, let's go inside," she says.

The prettiest and sweetest big sister

"Hey, there's my sweet Squirrel!"
Grandma shouts happily.
"We've missed you."
Grandma gives Squirrel a kiss.

Squirrel already
feels much better.
She helps Mommy
hand out the acorn
cookies.

Then, she and Bear get to open the presents for the baby.

She also puts away the cards,
and gathers all the presents neatly.

Then, she gives Baby
Squirrel her bottle.

Finally, she waves goodbye to all the visitors and, together with Mommy, puts the baby to bed.

When her little sister is asleep,
Squirrel cuddles up closely to Mommy.
Mommy strokes her head. "I'm very proud of you," Mommy says.
"You've been a great help today. Baby Squirrel is so lucky
to have such a **pretty and sweet big sister like you!**"